TURKEY ON THE LOOSE!

by Sylvie Wickstrom

Dial Books for Young Readers New York

Published by Dial Books for Young Readers
A Division of Penguin Books USA Inc.
375 Hudson Street
New York, New York 10014

Copyright © 1990 by Sylvie Wickstrom
Printed in Hong Kong by South China Printing Company (1988) Limited
First Edition
W
10 9 8 7 6 5 4 3 2 1
Library of Congress Cataloging in Publication Data
Wickstrom, Sylvie.
Turkey on the loose! / by Sylvie Wickstrom.
p.   cm.
Summary: A turkey gets loose in an apartment house
and creates havoc.
ISBN 0-8037-0818-1.—ISBN 0-8037-0820-3 (lib. bdg.)
1. Turkeys—Fiction. 2. Apartment houses—Fiction.
I. Title.   PZ7.W6295Tu 1990
[E]—dc20   89-26056   CIP   AC

The art for each picture consists of a pencil and watercolor painting,
which is scanner-separated and reproduced in full color.

For my Uncle Salomon

Turkey
on the
loose!

bonk!

Excuse us, Turkey on the loose!

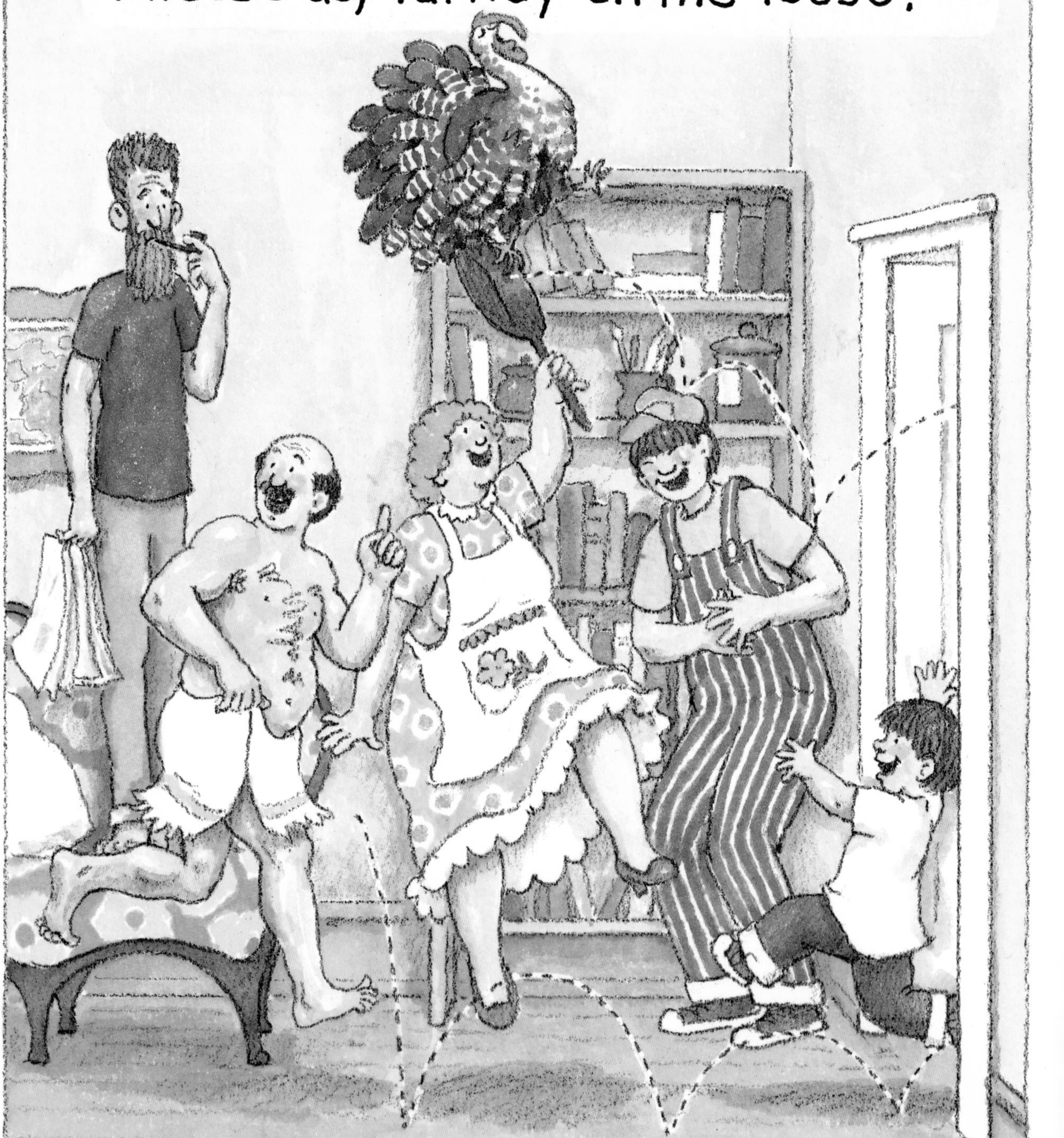

DATE DUE

FEB. 1 4 1992	NOV. 2 1 1994	
MAR. 0 6 1992	DEC. 0 7 1994	
APR. 0 6 1992	DEC. 0 7 1994	
JUN. 1 6 1992	MAR 3 1 1995	
JUL 2 7 1992	MAY 2 6 1995	
NOV. 2 7 1992	JUN 1 6 1995	
DEC. 1 4 1992	JUL 1 3 1995	
DEC. 3 1 1992	NOV. 2 9 1995	
FEB. 0 5 1993	OCT 0 2 1996	
AUG. 1 0 1993	DEC 1 1 1996	
	MAR 1 2 1997	
NOV. 1 0 1993	JUN 0 2 1997	
NOV. 2 9 1993	AUG 1 2 1997	
FEB 1994	SEP 0 8 1997	
JUL 1 4 1994	OCT 1 7 1997	
SEP. 3 0 1994		
OCT. 2 5 1994		
GAYLORD		PRINTED IN U.S.A.